Breakthrough Inventions

INVENTING THE AUTOMOBILE

Erinn Banting

Crabtree Publishing Company
www.crabtreebooks.com

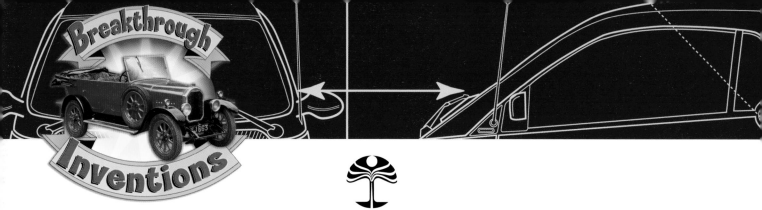

Crabtree Publishing Company
www.crabtreebooks.com

Coordinating editor: Ellen Rodger

Series and project editor: Adrianna Morganelli

Designer and production coordinator: Rosie Gowsell

Production assistant: Samara Parent

Scanning technician: Arlene Arch-Wilson

Art director: Rob MacGregor

Project development, editing, photo editing, and layout:
First Folio Resource Group, Inc.: Tom Dart, Sarah Gleadow,
Debbie Smith, Adam Wood

Photo research: Maria DeCambra

Consultants: Ron Barnett, Antique Automobile Club of America;
Jack Innes, President, The Canadian Automotive Museum; Tracy
Powell, *Automobile Quarterly*

Photographs: ALIX/Photo Researchers, Inc.: p. 28 (top); Justin
Allfree/istock International: p. 19 (top); AP/Wide World Photo:
p. 22 (top), p. 26 (bottom), p. 29 (top), p. 30 (bottom), p. 31 (top and
center); Austrian Archives/Corbis: p. 11; Bettmann/Corbis: p. 10
(top), p. 17; David Caton/Alamy: p. 14; David Cooper/Toronto
Star/firstlight.ca: p. 30 (top); Corbis: p. 6 (top); Granger Collection,
New York: p. 6 (bottom), p. 7 (top), p. 16 (bottom); George
Hall/Corbis: p. 25 (bottom); Hulton-Deutsch Collection/Corbis:
p. 5 (bottom), p. 7 (bottom), p. 10 (bottom); Jim Jurica/istock

International: p. 18; Helen King/Corbis: p. 19 (bottom); Lester
Lefkowitz/Getty Images: p. 25 (top); © 1981 Cindy Lewis: All
Rights Reserved.: p. 12; National Motor Museum/HIP/The Image
Works: p. 13 (top); National Motor Museum/Topham-HIP/The
Image Works: p. 23; Charles O'Rear/Corbis: p. 15;
Photodisc/firstlight.ca: p. 24; Reuters/Corbis: p. 28 (bottom);
Stapleton Collection/Corbis: p. 5 (top); Karen Town/istock
International: p. 26 (top); Tony Tremblay/istock International:
p. 22 (bottom); Alex Wong/Getty Images: p. 31 (bottom); David
Woods/Corbis: p. 27; Other images from stock photo CD.

Illustrations: Dan Kangas: title page, pp. 20–21;
www.mikecarterstudio.com: p. 3, p. 8, p. 9

Cover: The work of early inventors led to the development of the
car, which has improved many aspects of people's lives.

Title page: Early and modern cars have many similarities, but cars
today are much faster, come in many different models and colors,
and have many more features than the first cars.

Contents: Four-stroke internal combustion engines power most cars.

Crabtree Publishing Company
www.crabtreebooks.com   1-800-387-7650

Printed in the U.S.A./022011/WW20110117

Cataloging-in-Publication Data
Banting, Erinn.
    Inventing the automobile / written by Erinn Banting.
    p. cm. -- (Breakthrough inventions)
Includes index.
    ISBN-13: 978-0-7787-2812-2 (rlb)
    ISBN-10: 0-7787-2812-9 (rlb)
    ISBN-13: 978-0-7787-2834-4 (pb)
    ISBN-10: 0-7787-2834-X (pb)
    1. Automobiles--Design and construction--History--Juvenile
literature. 2. Inventions--History--Juvenile literature. I. Title. II. Series.
    TL147.B243 2006
    629.2'3109--dc22   2005034061
                                                         LC

Published in
the United States
PMB 59051
350 Fifth Avenue, 59th Floor
New York, New York 10118

Published
in Canada
616 Welland Ave.,
St. Catharines,
Ontario, Canada
L2M 5V6

Published in the
United Kingdom
Maritime House
Basin Road North, Hove
BN41 1WR
United Kingdom

Published
in Australia
386 Mt. Alexander Rd.,
Ascot Vale (Melbourne)
VIC 3032

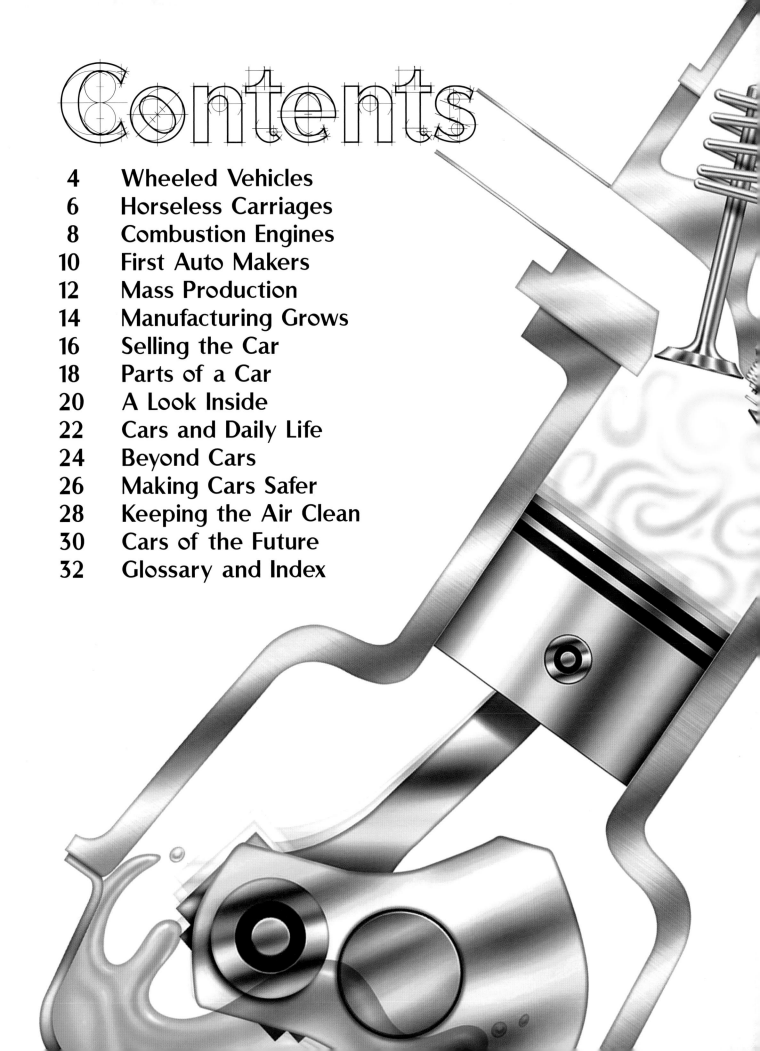

Contents

Wheeled Vehicles

The invention of the automobile has had an enormous impact on the world. People drive cars as a means of transportation, they rely on cars for their work, and they enjoy cars as a hobby. Worldwide, manufacturers build more than 30 million cars each year.

Life Before Wheeled Vehicles

Before wheeled vehicles, people traveled over land on foot or on animals, such as camels, horses, oxen, and donkeys. The poor conditions of the few roads made land travel very difficult. Rivers and lakes provided natural routes for rafts, boats, and ships.

On a Roll

The invention of the wheel improved land transportation by making it possible to roll goods over different types of **terrain**. Ancient Chinese drawings suggest the first wheel was built around 8000 B.C. The oldest wheel discovered by **archaeologists** was made around 3500 B.C. in Mesopotamia, which is an ancient region in present-day Iraq.

All methods of early transportation were sometimes dangerous. Watercraft could be damaged in storms, and animals could be injured or die on long journeys.

The language of ancient Rome was Latin. The Latin word for "chariot" is carra, which is the origin of the word "car."

Getting Around

People soon began to build carts, which had two wheels, and wagons, which had four wheels. Chariots were two-wheeled vehicles pulled by horses or camels. Fast and easy to steer, chariots transported people in Egypt, Greece, Rome, and India between 3000 B.C. and 1500 B.C., but they were too small to transport supplies.

The most common vehicle used to transport goods during the **Roman Empire** was the *plaustrum*. The *plaustrum* was made from a large plank of wood laid on two or four wheels, and was pulled by oxen.

From Carts to Coaches

During the **Middle Ages**, people in western Europe improved on the cart's design by adding steerable **axles**, which made turning easier. Iron springs and leather belts fastened between the axles and the frame absorbed some of the bumpiness of the ride. Passenger comfort improved with the invention of the coach, a vehicle with an enclosed seating area, pulled by horses.

Carriages were open vehicles that sometimes had fabric tops to protect the vehicles' occupants. People in large cities often hired carriages to take them from place to place.

ND. Phot.

2315

PARIS NOUVEAU — LES FEMMES COCHER
Mme Moser. — Au Bois, promenade du matin.

Horseless Carriages

To improve their speed and durability, early inventors attached steam engines or electric motors to the frames of carriages, which were previously pulled by animals. These early experiments led to the development of the car.

Picking up Steam

Early steam engines were powered by coal or wood. As the fuel burned, water boiled to create steam. The steam expanded, moving the engine and other parts of the vehicle. Nicolas-Joseph Cugnot, a member of the French army, built the first steam-powered vehicle in 1769, called the "steam wagon." It was used to carry large weapons, such as cannon, into battle.

(below) Nicolas-Joseph Cugnot's steam wagon was the first wheeled vehicle to move under its own power, but it had to be stopped every ten minutes to let the engine build up enough steam to keep it moving.

Full Steam Ahead!

European inventors built on Cugnot's work and made engines smaller and more efficient. Their vehicles could travel greater distances before having to stop to build up steam. Some vehicles were difficult to steer and control, which caused accidents, and the boilers, where steam was created, often exploded. Engines also **backfired**, creating loud noises that startled people. In countries such as England, vehicles powered by engines were considered so frightening and dangerous that the government passed laws restricting their use to private roads and property.

(above) Early motorized vehicles were nicknamed "horseless carriages." Many had seats in the front and platforms in the back on which drivers stood so they did not block passengers' views.

Steam Cars

As steam engines improved and as people began to build more cars to carry passengers and goods, cars gained popularity in Europe and North America. In the early 1900s, the De Dion Bouton, built by French mechanics George Bouton and Charles-Armand Trépardoux, was one of the most popular steam cars in Europe. The Stanley Steamer, built by American brothers Freelan and Francis Stanley, was popular in the United States.

Running on Electricity

Between 1880 and the early 1900s, electric cars, which were powered by batteries, were introduced in England, Europe, and North America. Electric cars did not backfire like steam cars, and they were less expensive to power, but they could only travel 50 miles (80 kilometers) before their batteries needed recharging. This made them inconvenient to use for long journeys.

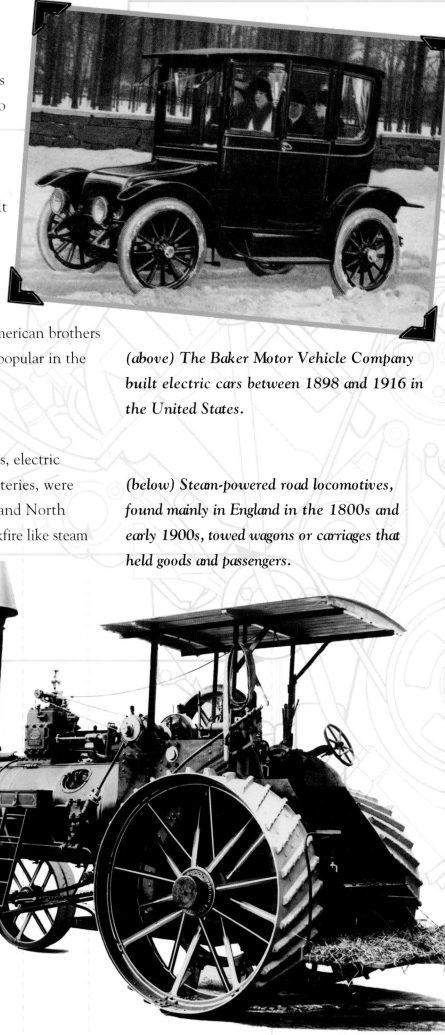

(above) The Baker Motor Vehicle Company built electric cars between 1898 and 1916 in the United States.

(below) Steam-powered road locomotives, found mainly in England in the 1800s and early 1900s, towed wagons or carriages that held goods and passengers.

Combustion Engines

To further improve a vehicle's speed and efficiency, many inventors experimented with internal combustion engines, which are powered by burning a mixture of air and gasoline within cylinders. The success of their experiments forever changed the car.

The Internal Combustion Engine

American inventor Samuel Morey designed one of the first internal combustion engines in the early 1800s. He received a **patent** for the engine in 1826, but never built one that worked well. The internal combustion engine burned fuel, such as kerosene or turpentine. When the fuel was heated and mixed with air, it combusted, or exploded, in a chamber at the top of the cylinder. This created pressure that caused a piston to move up and down inside the cylinder. The piston's movement pushed the mixture of fuel and air through the cylinder to power the engine. It also pushed **exhaust** out of the cylinder.

The Two-Stroke Engine

In 1859, Belgian-born inventor Étienne Lenoir built the first internal combustion engine that powered a car. It operated on two strokes, which are upward or downward movements of the piston. In 1863, Lenoir built a car around one of his engines, but the engine was not powerful enough to make the car run reliably.

A Modern Two-Stroke Engine

Here is how a modern two-stroke engine works:

Stroke 1: The piston moves down, pushing exhaust out of the cylinder and pulling in a mixture of fuel and air.

Stroke 2: The piston moves up, compressing the mixture of fuel and air. A **spark plug** fires and ignites the mixture, and the explosion pushes the piston back down.

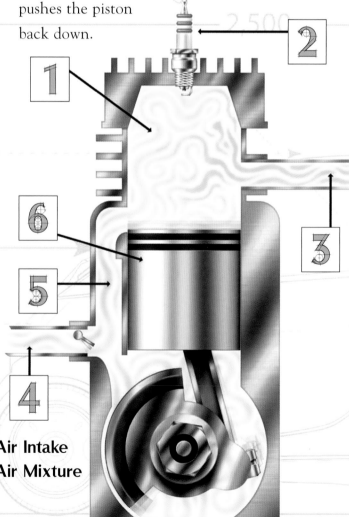

1. **Combustion Chamber**
2. **Spark Plug**
3. **Exhaust Outlet**
4. **Fuel and Air Intake**
5. **Fuel and Air Mixture**
6. **Piston**

The Four-Stroke Engine

German engineer Nikolaus Otto, with his partners Gottlieb Daimler and Wilhelm Maybach, built the first working four-stroke engine in 1876. The four-stroke engine was much easier to run than the two-stroke engine and was able to power a vehicle successfully.

A Modern Four-Stroke Engine

Here is how a modern four-stroke engine works:

Stroke 1: The piston pushes down, pulling a mixture of fuel and air into the cylinder.

Stroke 2: The piston moves up, compressing the mixture at the top of the cylinder.

Stroke 3: A spark from the spark plug ignites the mixture, and the pressure caused by the explosion pushes the piston down.

Stroke 4: The piston is forced back up to release the exhaust.

1. Exhaust Outlet
2. Exhaust Valve
3. Spark Plug
4. Intake Valve
5. Fuel and Air Intake
6. Fuel and Air Mixture
7. Piston

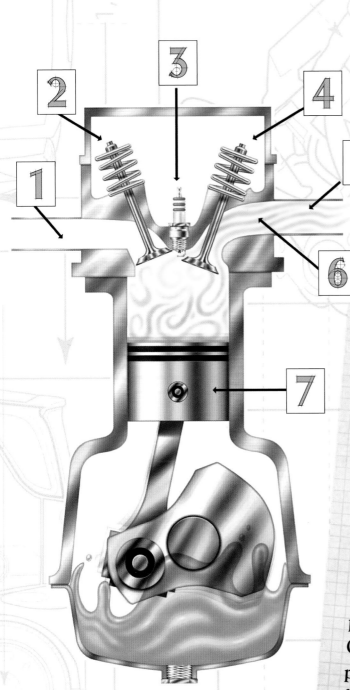

Patent Controversy

Disputes over patents happened regularly when the first cars were built. Nikolaus Otto is considered the first person to build a four-stroke internal combustion engine, but French engineer Alphonse Beau de Rochas had already patented the idea in 1862 — 14 years before Otto built his engine. In 1886, after more than 30,000 engines had been built based on Otto's model, Otto's right to de Rochas's patent was revoked, or taken back, and Otto was forced to pay de Rochas a percentage of the money he earned from the engines he sold.

First Auto Makers

I n the late 1800s and early 1900s, the main goal of people developing cars was to make vehicles that actually worked. As a result of their experimentation, technology changed so quickly that new models became obsolete, or outdated, soon after they were introduced.

Karl Benz

German engineer Karl Benz built a motorized tricycle that was powered by a four-stroke internal combustion engine in 1885. The tricycle, called the *Motorwagen*, reached speeds of up to eight miles (13 kilometers) per hour.

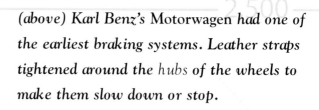

(above) Karl Benz's Motorwagen *had one of the earliest braking systems. Leather straps tightened around the* hubs *of the wheels to make them slow down or stop.*

(above) Gottlieb Daimler and Wilhelm Maybach's first vehicle reached speeds of up to 12 miles (19 kilometers) per hour.

Daimler and Maybach

In 1886, German engineers Gottlieb Daimler and Wilhelm Maybach attached a four-stroke engine to the back of a carriage frame, and created the first workable car. The driver sat at the front and steered the vehicle with a **tiller**. The vehicle also had a four-speed gearbox. The gears helped move the wheels faster without increasing the speed of the engine, which prevented the engine from overheating or exploding. To shift gears, drivers had to stop their cars and then start them again to continue their journeys.

Daimler-Benz

In 1890, Daimler and Maybach founded the Daimler Motor Company. They introduced the Mercedes, a line of cars still built today. The Mercedes had many new features, including radiators, which helped cool engines, and smaller steel frames, which made the cars lighter so they traveled more quickly. In 1926, the Daimler Motor Company joined Karl Benz's company, Benz & Co., to form Daimler-Benz. Daimler-Benz built the first **diesel** car in 1936. Its engine, invented by Rudolph Diesel in 1890, was more powerful and efficient than other types of engines.

Panhard-Levassor

French engineers René Panhard and Emile Levassor built their first car in 1891. The vehicle was powered by a Daimler engine placed under the hood at the front, not in the back as in earlier cars. Four years later, they introduced the first **transmission** with a clutch, in their Panhard car. For the first time, drivers could change gears while the car was still moving.

Workers at the Daimler Motor Company paint cars in this photograph from 1904. Today, the company is known as Mercedes-Benz.

Mass Production

As the demand for cars increased, the number and size of auto plants in Europe and North America grew. Factories improved the manufacturing process, making it faster and less expensive to build cars. With these changes, cars became more affordable for the average person.

The Assembly Line

Early cars were built one at a time and entirely by hand. The assembly sometimes took more than a year, which made cars very expensive and affordable only to the wealthy. In 1901, American automobile manufacturer Ransom Eli Olds installed an assembly line in his auto plant, Olds Motor Works. Workers moved from car to car to install a piece or system, which sped up the manufacturing process. Olds also began using parts built by other manufacturers, instead of having his factory manufacture all the parts. After introducing these changes, production costs decreased and car production increased.

Henry Ford

When Henry Ford founded the Ford Motor Company in 1903, his goal was to build cars that were affordable, mechanically reliable, and long lasting. In 1913, Ford introduced the first moving assembly line at his factory in Dearborn, Michigan. Workers no longer had to move from car to car to add their parts. Instead, the cars traveled to the workers along conveyor belts. Ford's moving assembly line allowed workers to build a car in 93 minutes, compared to the days, or even weeks, other car manufacturers required. Reducing the time it took to build cars and increasing production lowered the cost of cars.

One of the first widely sold cars in the United States was the curved-dash Oldsmobile, manufactured by Olds Motor Works.

(above) Between 1908 and 1927, Ford's assembly line built more than 15 million cars.

(below) Early Ford models were named after letters of the alphabet. Ford's first popular car was the Model T, built between 1908 and 1928.

Shift Work

Demand for cars increased as the prices of cars decreased. To keep up with the demand, Henry Ford divided the workday into a day shift and a night shift. Each shift used different employees. This way, Ford's manufacturing plants could build cars into the night without exhausting workers. Ford also doubled the average salary he paid his workers compared to workers in other car factories. Ford's changes improved conditions for workers in other industries as well, who argued that they wanted to be treated as well as employees of Ford.

Manufacturing Grows

Once assembly lines became common, many more car manufacturers became profitable. Car manufacturing grew to be one of the largest industries in the world. Many car manufacturers that opened in the early 1900s still build cars today.

BMW

German manufacturer BMW was formed in 1916 as Bayerische Flugzeugwerke, a company that made aircraft engines. By 1928, BMW was building cars that became known for their high speed and **endurance**. Today, BMW manufactures luxury and sports cars, as well as motorcycles, under its own name and under the names of companies it has purchased. These include the luxury car manufacturer Rolls-Royce.

With the introduction of the electric starter, Cadillac sales climbed from 10,000 in 1911 to 14,000 in 1912.

General Motors

In 1908, an American businessman named William Crapo Durant created a car company called General Motors (GM) by buying many small- and medium-sized car companies, including Olds Motor Works. GM introduced new features to cars, including electric starters, which debuted in the 1912 Cadillac. Electric starters replaced the cranks, or handles, that people had to use to start their cars. Today, GM manufactures cars under lines such as Cadillac, Buick, Pontiac, Chevrolet, Saturn, and Hummer.

1769	**1876**	**1890**	**1901**	**1908**	**1912**	**1928**
Nicolas-Joseph Cugnot builds the first steam vehicle.	Nikolaus Otto builds the first four-stroke internal combustion engine.	Rudolph Diesel patents the diesel engine.	The assembly line is first used.	Electric headlights are first installed on cars.	The electric starter is introduced in GM's Cadillac.	Brakes on all four wheels become standard on most cars.

Chrysler

Walter P. Chrysler took over the Maxwell Motor Company factory in 1923 and, the following year, renamed it the Chrysler Corporation. Over the next 80 years, the Chrysler Corporation grew to be one of the largest car manufacturers in the United States. Among its most influential innovations was the minivan, introduced in 1984. Minivans, which have extra seats and room in the interior to make passengers more comfortable, are a popular mode of transportation for families. In 1998, Chrysler merged with Daimler-Benz and became Daimler-Chrysler.

Modern assembly lines use robots to do many of the tasks that people once did. Robots increase the efficiency of factories, enabling them to build more cars.

Toyota

The Toyota Motor Corporation was established in Japan in 1933, and became one of the country's largest car manufacturers in the 1960s and 1970s. Toyota's efficient, compact engines burned much less fuel than other cars at the time. The company's later innovations include a **hybrid** car called the Prius, which is more fuel-efficient than other types of cars.

Honda

The Honda Motor Company, established in 1946, began as the Honda Technical Research Institute. The Japanese company built small, efficient internal combustion engines, and, later, motorcycles and cars. The cars, made with **fiberglass** bodies, were lightweight and **aerodynamic**, so they moved faster than many other cars at the time.

1940	**1954**	**1964**	**1973**	**1984**	**1997**	**2004**
The first cars with automatic transmissions are built.	The first robot is installed on a U.S. assembly line.	Seat belts become mandatory in all cars.	Air bags are introduced.	The minivan is introduced.	The first commercially successful hybrid car is sold in Japan.	The smart fortwo car is introduced in North America.

Selling the Car

Early manufacturers tried many strategies to convince people to buy cars. They advertised in newspapers, held car races to attract public interest, and improved the performance, style, comfort, and safety of automobiles.

On Your Mark! Get Set! Go!

Car races gave manufacturers a way to test and display their new models and inventions, and they were exciting for spectators. During the first car race, which was held on public roads in 1894, 102 contestants raced between Paris and Rouen, in France. Beginning in 1927, Italian car manufacturers, such as Lancia, Alfa Romeo, Maserati, and Ferrari, entered their cars in the Mille Miglia, a race through Italy's mountains that began and ended in Rome.

(above) The Indy 500 is one of the most popular car races today. More than 250,000 spectators visit Indianapolis, in the United States, to watch the race each year.

(below) In this photograph from the 1920s, a driver races against an airplane. Races with airplanes demonstrated the speed that cars could reach.

The Indy 500

Danger to spectators, racers, and livestock caused public road races to decrease in number. In 1908, American businessman Carl G. Fisher began building the first U.S. racetrack in Indianapolis. Three years later, more than 80,000 spectators came to watch the first race. It was known as the Indy 500: "Indy" because it took place in Indianapolis and "500" because drivers had to race 500 miles (805 kilometers), which was 200 laps around the track.

Feeling Comfortable

Beginning around 1913, many companies began building cars with interiors that were elaborately decorated in wool, silk, and **ivory**. They hoped that the added comforts would increase sales. Over time, other features were added to make cars more comfortable and enjoyable to drive, including heating and air conditioning systems, radios, and CD and DVD players.

Sales of cars also increased with additional safety features. Windshields, bumpers, rearview mirrors, and locks were offered as optional features, and are now standard on all cars. Newer safety features include car alarms and global positioning system (GPS) devices, which show drivers their positions on the road and suggest the best routes to reach their destinations.

An advertisement for a car by the R-C-H Corporation lists the features and improvements to passenger safety, comfort, and price.

Dynamic Obsolescence

Between the early 1920s and late 1940s, world events such as the **Great Depression** and **World War II** made it difficult for car manufacturers to stay in business. To ensure his company did not go bankrupt, GM president Alfred P. Sloan came up with an idea he called dynamic obsolescence. Each year after a car was introduced, GM improved the design of the vehicle, until it became obsolete. Sloan argued that the changes made cars look better and run more smoothly. His critics accused Sloan of making people feel that they had to buy the latest cars, which would result in GM earning more money. In spite of the criticism, other car manufacturers soon adopted Alfred P. Sloan's idea.

Parts of a Car

Many parts, including the engine, lubrication system, fuel system, transmission, and brakes, work together to help a car run. The first cars had fewer than 50 parts, while cars today have thousands.

The Engine

The engine is the most important part of the car. Today, most cars are powered by gas engines, while many construction vehicles, trucks, and some automobiles are powered by diesel engines. Diesel engines use diesel fuel, a cheaper and less refined fuel than gasoline. Diesel fuel burns slightly longer than gasoline and creates more power. Some vehicles are powered by hybrid engines, which rely on a combination of sources, such as gasoline and battery-powered motors. Hybrid engines are more fuel-efficient than other types of engines.

Transmission

Cars have either manual or automatic transmissions. In a car with a manual transmission, the driver uses a clutch and gearshift to change gears. An automatic transmission shifts gears automatically, depending on how fast or slow the car is being driven. When a car reaches the maximum speed for a particular gear, the transmission shifts into a higher gear. When a car slows down, the transmission shifts into a lower gear.

(above) A car's lubrication system oils metal parts so they do not wear out quickly. The oil needs to be changed approximately every 4,000 miles (6,000 kilometers).

Fuel System

In early cars, gravity helped move fuel from the fuel tank to the engine. When driving uphill, cars often stopped because the fuel could not reach the engine. Cars had to be turned around, so the fuel tanks were above the engines, and driven in reverse. Modern cars rely on fuel-injection systems to suck the right amount of fuel from fuel tanks, mix it with air, and inject it into the engines' cylinders.

(right) Gears help cars reach maximum speeds using minimum power.

Brakes

There are two main kinds of brakes. Drum brakes are large drums, or cylinders, with metal blocks, called brake shoes, inside. They fit in cars' wheels. When the brake pedal is pressed, the brake shoes push against the inside of the drums, slowing or stopping the wheels. Disc brakes are like the brakes on a bicycle. When a driver presses on the brake pedal, calipers, which are like clamps, squeeze against discs. This slows down or stops the wheels.

A mechanic fixes a car's brakes. Many cars today have antilock brakes. Antilock brakes prevent the wheels from locking up when a driver slams on the brakes, so that the car does not skid on wet or slippery roads.

A Look Inside

A car's exterior consists mainly of a body, wheels, windows, and lights. Inside, cars are made up of thousands of parts that help them run smoothly and safely.

1. Battery: The battery supplies power to the car's starting system, computer, lights, and all other electric parts. An alternator keeps the battery charged.

2. Ignition switch: Turning the key in the ignition switch unlocks the steering wheel and sends electrical power to most of a car's accessories, such as the lights and radio. Turning it further feeds electrical power to the starting system, so the car can start.

3. Accelerator pedal: The accelerator pedal sends a message to the fuel-injection system, letting the car know how much fuel needs to be burned for it to run at different speeds.

4. Steering wheel: Turning a steering wheel in an older car required a lot of effort. Power steering, introduced in 1951, made steering faster and more accurate.

5. Shift lever: In a car with an automatic transmission, the shift lever allows the driver to shift from "Park" into "Reverse," "Neutral," or "Drive." It also allows a driver to move into first or second gear when going up or down steep slopes, to prevent the engine from overworking, or the brakes from wearing out too quickly.

6. Muffler: Mufflers help absorb noise made by the exhaust. A pipe leading from the muffler directs the exhaust out the back of the car.

7. Body: Most car bodies are made of steel, with trim made of plastic. The roof, rear, and sides of the car are usually reinforced with extra steel framework pieces, which better protect the vehicle's occupants during a collision.

8. Tires: Tires transfer power from the engine to the road. Different tires have **treads** designed to operate over different road surfaces and conditions.

9. Suspension system: The two main parts of the suspension system are the springs and the shock absorbers, or shocks. The springs allow wheels to move over bumps without causing the rest of the car to move too much. The shocks keep the car from bouncing when it hits a bump.

10. Lights: Exterior lights, including headlights, taillights, brake lights, and signal lights, help drivers see roads and other cars at night. They also indicate to other drivers whether cars are slowing down, stopping, or turning.

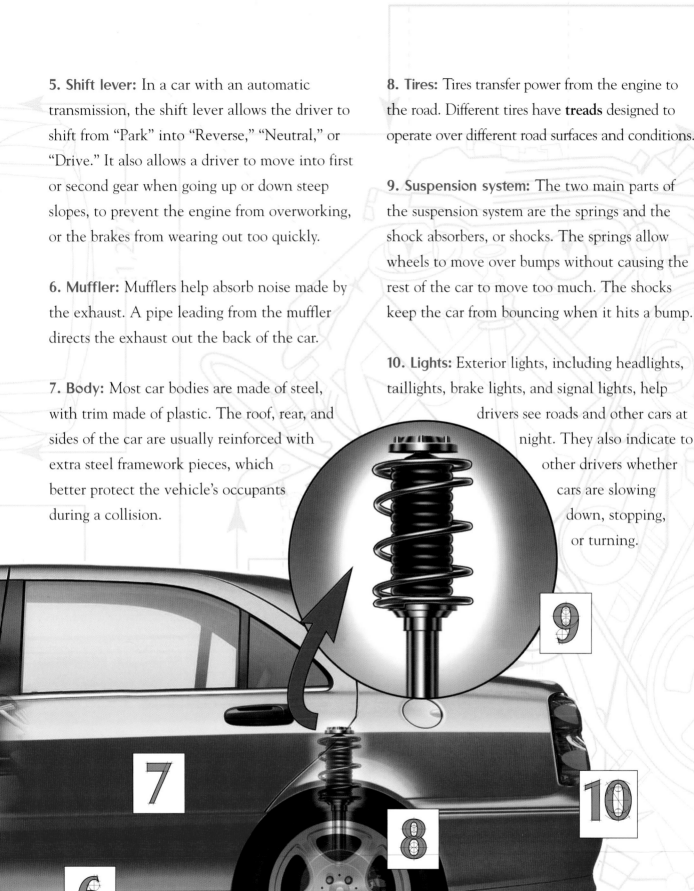

Cars and Daily Life

Today, people rely on cars on a daily basis. Their widespread use has changed the way roads and cities are built, created new industries, and led to thousands of laws that protect drivers and pedestrians.

Riding the Roads

Early roads were made of dirt or were covered in cobblestones or gravel. When cars became more common, paved roadways, which were safer and lasted longer, were built. The first paved roadways were constructed in England with layers of stone chips and tar rolled flat. Today, many roads are made with a mixture of tar and gravel.

Highways

Highway surfaces are often made of concrete, which is more durable than tar and gravel. Highways were first built in European countries such as Germany and Italy in the 1930s. The roads, which connected major cities, had higher speed limits and multiple lanes that could hold more traffic. By the 1940s, the United States, Canada, and England also built highways. As highways developed, cities and suburbs grew because people could live farther away from where they worked.

(above) Car clubs organize events that bring together people who want to buy, repair, sell, share stories, or learn more about particular types of cars.

(left) In the United States, people drive more than 1.3 trillion miles (2.09 trillion kilometers) each year, which equals more than one billion trips around the world.

In the early 1900s, when cars did not have roofs or sides, women wore wide-brimmed hats with veils and men wore large goggles and hats to protect themselves from wind, rain, snow, or strong sunshine.

New Industries

The popularity of cars has allowed other industries to grow. Millions of manufacturers build parts for cars, including bodies, engines, and tires. Service stations, which began as small roadside sheds, sell gas, perform minor repairs, and sell beverages, snacks, and other items people need while traveling. Other companies publish maps, manufacture games that children play during car trips, design advertisements for roadside billboards, or sell **insurance** to drivers.

Laws for Drivers

As the number of cars on roads increased, new laws were needed to protect pedestrians and drivers. England's Red Flag Law was one of the earliest traffic laws. Until 1904, the Red Flag Law required a driver to have a person carry a red flag in front of the car to warn others that a vehicle was approaching. Today, traffic laws regulate everything from who can drive to how fast they can drive.

Beyond Cars

The success and popularity of cars paved the way for other means of land transportation. Today, a wide range of vehicles is built, and vehicles are modified for specific needs.

A Variety of Vehicles

Car manufacturers have introduced vehicles such as minivans, recreational vehicles (RVs), and sport-utility vehicles (SUVs) to meet the needs of their customers. Minivans give drivers more room to transport their families safely and comfortably. RVs, which include sleeping quarters, washrooms, and kitchens, are used for camping. SUVs are combinations of cars and four-wheel drive trucks. They have a lot of room for passengers and equipment, and can be easily driven in mud, in snow, or on rough terrain.

Adapted Vehicles

Many cars, vans, and buses can be adapted so that people with disabilities are able to drive and ride in them. Minivans can be equipped with ramps for easier access, and the floors can be lowered so that people in wheelchairs can drive from their chairs. Hand controls replace accelerator and brake pedals in vehicles whose drivers have limited use of their legs. Power steering can be adjusted so that it is easier for people with limited movement in their hands to steer.

Automated ramps on public buses make it easier for people with disabilities to board and exit.

Delivery Trucks

Before the early 1900s, horse-drawn wagons delivered groceries and supplies from local farms and factories to people's homes. Today, goods are delivered by transport trucks, which have special features to ensure the items they carry arrive safely. Many trucks have ramps to help with loading and unloading, and bars to keep goods from moving. Trucks that carry animals have openings so that fresh air can circulate, as well as drinking facilities and space to store animal feed. "Sleeper" trucks are built with beds, televisions, and toilets so that drivers can rest during long journeys.

(right) Transport trucks load and unload their cargo. Trucks transporting food that must be refrigerated or frozen have insulated floors, walls, and ceilings to keep food from spoiling.

Emergency Vehicles

Before cars were invented, doctors, firefighters, and police traveled to people's homes on foot, by horse, by horse-drawn carriage, or by bicycle. These early forms of transportation were slow and often did not arrive in time. Today, vehicles such as police cars, ambulances, and fire engines are used for emergencies.

Police cars are modified so that they can be driven faster than other vehicles in emergency situations. They have more powerful engines and brakes, and very efficient transmission, suspension, and cooling systems. Ambulances are designed to have room in the back for two or more patients, and for emergency medical technicians (EMTs) or paramedics to care for them. Ambulances also carry equipment and supplies for emergency care, and sometimes, light rescue equipment.

Fire engines are equipped with tanks that have water and foam for extinguishing fires. They also have hoses, water pumps, and pump panels, used to control which hoses have water flowing through them, and how much.

Making Cars Safer

Early cars did not have many of the safety features that today's cars have, such as turn signals, mirrors, bumpers, and shatterproof glass. In addition to these features, cars today are built with crumple zones, seat belts, and air bags to protect drivers and passengers in case of collisions.

The Seat Belt

Seat belts, first installed by Nash Motors in 1949, are one of the most important safety features of cars today, but they were not mandatory in cars until the mid-1960s. Early seat belts crossed over people's hips, which held them in their seats during collisions, but did not prevent their heads from hitting dashboards or windshields. In 1959, Nihls Bolin, an engineer at Swedish car manufacturer Volvo, invented the three-point seat belt. A three-point seat belt has one strap across the lap and a second diagonal strap across the chest to better hold passengers in place.

Crumple Zones

In 1959, Bela Berenyi, an engineer at Mercedes-Benz, introduced crumple zones in the front and rear of most of the company's cars. These zones absorb the shock of a collision and crumple so that passengers are not injured. Berenyi also improved side impact beams, which absorb the shock if cars are hit on the side.

(above) In many parts of the world, it is illegal to be in a car without a seat belt.

(below) Crumple zones, along with the use of stronger materials, reduce the risk of injury during a collision.

2003 SAAB 93
INSURANCE INSTITUTE
FOR HIGHWAY SAFETY
CEF0306

Air Bags

In 1952, American inventor John Hetrick developed the idea for air bags, which are safety cushions built into steering wheels, dashboards, doors, and seats. When cars are hit head-on or on the sides, the air bags inflate and reduce the impact of crashes on drivers and passengers. Early air bags sometimes harmed a vehicle's occupants because they inflated so quickly and with such force. Today, with the help of computers, air bags deploy to different sizes at different speeds, depending on the severity of the crash.

Car Seats

The first child car seats, invented in the 1930s, held children still while cars were moving, but did not protect them in collisions. In 1960, designers at Volvo improved the car seat by adding two diagonal belts that held children in place, and prevented them from being thrown forward in collisions. Volvo later designed a seat that faced backward, further protecting children during head-on collisions.

Crash Tests

To test how safe cars are, manufacturers perform safety tests, or crash tests. Early crash tests were performed in the 1930s to measure the damage done to cars when they crashed at different speeds. In the 1950s, crash test dummies were added to safety tests to see what impact collisions had on human beings. Today, there are crash test dummies made to the height and weight of the average man, woman, child, and even dog.

Cars are given crash test scores. Five stars indicate the most protection, one star the least.

Keeping the Air Clean

Cars have improved many aspects of people's lives, but they have also threatened the environment. They use up natural resources, cause pollution, and fill landfill sites. Car manufacturers are looking for ways to reduce the damage, and commuters help by taking public transit or car pooling.

(above) Cyclists in large cities often wear anti-pollution masks to protect themselves from vehicle emissions.

(right) Battery-powered electric cars, which were popular in the early 1900s, are being built again because they produce very little pollution. Some shopping malls have outlets where drivers of electric cars can recharge their vehicles' batteries.

Alternative Fuels

Scientists and car manufacturers are experimenting with alternative ways of powering cars. Biodiesel and ethanol are fuels made from plants, which are **renewable** resources. They release fewer harmful emissions than gasoline. In some major cities, diesel buses are being replaced with buses that use fuel cells. Fuel cells mix gasoline, natural gas, propane, methanol, or other **hydrogen**-rich fuels with oxygen, and convert the mixture to electricity and heat. Water is the only emission from a fuel cell. Car manufacturers are also developing improved hybrid cars.

The World Solar Challenge is a 1,870-mile (3,010-kilometer) car race that takes place in Australia every other year. Solar-powered cars have panels on their roofs that use the sun's energy to charge their batteries. The batteries then supply power to the engines.

Problems with Pollution

The emissions, or pollutants, released by cars, and the **Freon** used in cars' air-conditioning systems, contribute to air pollution and the **greenhouse effect**. Many countries have passed strict emissions laws. Older cars must be tested regularly for excess emissions of carbon monoxide and other harmful gases. Cars that fail the test must have their exhaust systems and engines adjusted before the vehicles can be driven again.

Recycling Helps

In the past, tires, metal, and plastic from scrapped cars have gone into garbage dumps and landfill sites. Recently, programs have been developed to encourage recycling. Rubber tires are shredded into small chips and turned into asphalt, which is used to pave roads. Cars are shredded into small pieces, which are separated into glass, steel, plastic, rubber, and chemicals. These materials are individually recycled or made into new parts for cars. Harmful substances, such as **antifreeze**, battery acid, brake fluid, and oil, which can seep into the soil and enter waterways, are removed before cars are recycled.

Plastic, used in a car's interior, can take up to 100 years to decompose, or break down. Aluminum, used on the car's exterior and in its engine, can take up to 300 years.

Cars of the Future

Concept cars, nicknamed "dream cars," are prototypes that are built using the latest technology and designs. Automakers use them to demonstrate innovations in car design and to measure the public's reaction to new features.

The smart fortwo ▶

Mercedes-Benz introduced the smart fortwo car in Europe in 1998 and in North America in 2004. The car, which seats two people, is only eight feet (2.5 meters) long and five feet (1.5 meters) wide. Originally designed for crowded city streets, smart fortwo cars are so small they can be parked either beside the curb or facing it. The car's three-cylinder diesel engine is also extremely fuel-efficient.

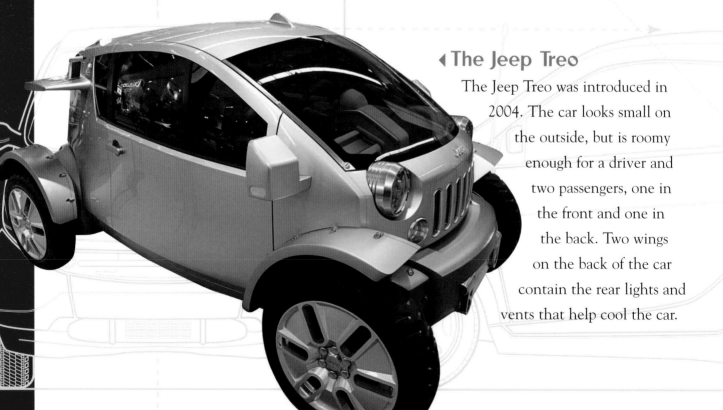

◀ The Jeep Treo

The Jeep Treo was introduced in 2004. The car looks small on the outside, but is roomy enough for a driver and two passengers, one in the front and one in the back. Two wings on the back of the car contain the rear lights and vents that help cool the car.

Toyota PM ▶

The Toyota PM, which stands for Personal Mobility, was introduced in 2003. The PM seats one person, and does not have side doors. The driver enters through a hatch that holds the bubble-shaped windshield. When the hatch closes, the seat reclines to make the ride more comfortable.

◀ The Lotus Elise

Introduced as a compact sports car in 1995, the Lotus Elise is only 12.5 feet (3.8 meters) long. Made with aluminum, a lightweight metal, it is one of the fastest sports cars for a car its weight, able to accelerate to more than 100 miles per hour (185 kilometers per hour) in just 13.5 seconds.

The Mercedes-Benz Bionic ▼

Mercedes-Benz looked to science and nature for their 2005 Bionic concept car. Engineers built the car frame based on the bone structure of the boxfish, a tropical fish that moves quickly through water despite its boxy shape. Lightweight, aerodynamic, and powered by a diesel engine, the car is 20 to 30 percent more fuel efficient than other cars of similar size.

Glossary

aerodynamic Designed with round edges to move more easily through strong winds

antifreeze A liquid added to a car's cooling system to allow it to operate in low temperatures

archaeologist A person who studies the past by examining buildings and artifacts

axle A long bar on which wheels turn

backfire To explode and make a loud noise, such as when fuel ignites too soon

cylinder The chamber in which a piston moves

diesel A type of fuel that is ignited by heat from compressed air, rather than by an electrical spark

endurance The ability to remain in good working condition over a period of continued use

exhaust Fumes and gases that are released as fuel is used up

fiberglass A material made from glass fibers, or threads

Freon A chemical compound used in refrigeration and air conditioning systems

Great Depression A period of mass unemployment and poverty in the 1930s

greenhouse effect The warming of the Earth's surface due to pollution in the atmosphere

hub The central part of a wheel

hybrid A vehicle whose engine uses more than one source of power

hydrogen A colorless, odorless gas

insulate To prevent heat from entering or leaving an area by surrounding it with a special material

insurance Money paid to a driver in the event of a collision or theft, to compensate for damages

ivory A white bone-like substance from the tusks of animals such as elephants

Middle Ages The period from about 500 A.D. to 1500 A.D. in western Europe

natural resource A material found in nature, such as oil or coal

patent A legal document that prevents people from using inventors' ideas for a certain period of time without giving them proper recognition and payment

prototype The first full-size, usually working model of an invention

renewable Able to be used continuously without running out

Roman Empire A group of territories under the control of Rome from 27 B.C. to 395 A.D.

spark plug A device that produces a spark to ignite the fuel mixture in a gasoline engine

terrain The features of land in a particular area

tiller A handle used to steer

transmission Gears and other car parts that transmit, or send, power from the engine to the wheels

tread The part of a tire that touches the road

World War II A war fought by countries around the world from 1939 to 1945

Index